LITTLE CHICK

This Little Chick book
belongs to:

LITTLE CHICK

BY AMY HEST

WITH PICTURES BY ANITA JERAM

WALKER BOOKS
AND SUBSIDIARIES
LONDON • BOSTON • SYDNEY • AUCKLAND

For Lon always A.H.

For Olivia, Bobby and Max A.J.

First published 2009 by Walker Books Ltd
87 Vauxhall Walk, London SE11 5HJ

This edition published 2010

2 4 6 8 10 9 7 5 3 1

This book has been typeset in Godlike

Printed in China

British Library Cataloguing in Publication Data:
a catalogue record for this book is available from the British Library

ISBN 978-1-4063-2535-5

www.walker.co.uk

Three Stories about Little Chick

The Carrot That Would Not Grow

One morning

Little Chick hopped across the grass.

She hopped right to the

edge of her garden.

And that's where

she sat, waiting for

her carrot to grow.

Before long, Old-Auntie crossed the lawn. She stopped at the edge of the garden and whispered, "Good morning, Little Chick."

“Good morning, Old-Auntie,”
Little Chick whispered back.
“I am waiting for my
carrot to grow.”

"You are a good and patient gardener,"
observed Old-Auntie.
"Yes," agreed Little Chick.
"I am a good and patient gardener."

Old-Auntie sat down, and together they
waited for Little Chick's carrot to grow.

It did not grow.

They waited
some more ...

and some more ...

and still it did not grow.

Little Chick sighed.

"I want my carrot to be tall," she said,

and leaned against Old-Auntie.

"A tall carrot is certainly nice,"

agreed Old-Auntie.

"But sometimes,"

she whispered, "a *small*

carrot is just what you need."

Little Chick looked
at her carrot that
would not grow.
It was very small ...

and she needed
it very much ...

so she pulled it ...

out of

the ground!

Little Chick showed her carrot
to Old-Auntie.

"Some carrots are tall, and some
are not," observed Old-Auntie.
"But in all my years,
I have never seen a carrot
as beautiful as that."

"Thank you," said Little Chick,
and then she kissed Old-Auntie.

And together they sat
at the edge of the garden,
admiring Little Chick's
beautiful carrot.

The Kite That Would Not Fly

The sun was hot,

the grass was green and Little Chick skipped across the garden, pulling her kite on a string.

"Fly!" she sang. "Up to the sky!"

But Little Chick's kite would not fly...

It bobbed on green grass
and dragged behind.

Along came Old-Auntie
to cheer her on.
"Good afternoon, Little Chick."

"Good afternoon, Old-Auntie."
Little Chick skipped
a bit faster.
"Fly!" she sang.

"You are skipping very nicely,"
observed Old-Auntie.
"Yes," agreed Little Chick.
"I skip very nicely."

But still her kite
would not fly...

It bobbed on green grass
and dragged behind.

Little Chick sighed.
She was tired of skipping very nicely.
She was tired of a kite that dragged.
So she stopped right there
and leaned against Old-Auntie.
"I want my kite to fly," she said.

Old-Auntie bent all the way down
and kissed Little Chick.
"Sometimes a kite will fly,"
observed Old-Auntie,
"and sometimes it simply *won't*."

Little Chick felt sad.
"Come along, kite," she said.

And she pulled the string and walked
very slowly up the big hill
with Old-Auntie.

It was windy on the hill,

and they were high high up.

Whoosh!

went the wind.

Whooosh!

Little Chick skipped with

the wind in her face.

She skipped fast
across the hill
. . . faster and
faster still.

Whoosh!

went the wind.

Whooosh!

And up went her kite ...

up ...

up ...

into the sky.

The Starry Night

Soon it would be night.

High in the sky, the first star
popped up, bright and beautiful.

Little Chick stood on the step.
"Reach for the sky!" she sang.

She stretched

and stretched,

trying to catch

her star.

Just then Old-Auntie
came by and whispered,
"Good evening, Little Chick."

"Good evening, Old-Auntie,"
Little Chick whispered back.
"I need to catch my star!
I want to put it in my pocket!"

Little Chick stretched very high.
"You are a good stretcher,"
said Old-Auntie.
"Yes," agreed Little Chick.
"I am a good stretcher."
She stretched higher
and higher still.

She could not catch her star.

Her pocket was empty.

Little Chick felt sad.

"I want my star," she said.

"It is *such* a lovely star,"
observed Old-Auntie.
"I love the way it sparkles."
"Yes," agreed Little Chick. "It sparkles."
"I'm afraid the sky just wouldn't be
the same without your star," said
Old-Auntie. "It would be rather *dull*."
"Yes," agreed Little Chick.
"It would be dull."

Little Chick and Old-Auntie

left the star in the sky.

When the sky was blue velvet,

more stars popped up.

More and more and more!

Little Chick's star was the loveliest of all.

Other Books by Amy Hest and Anita Jeram

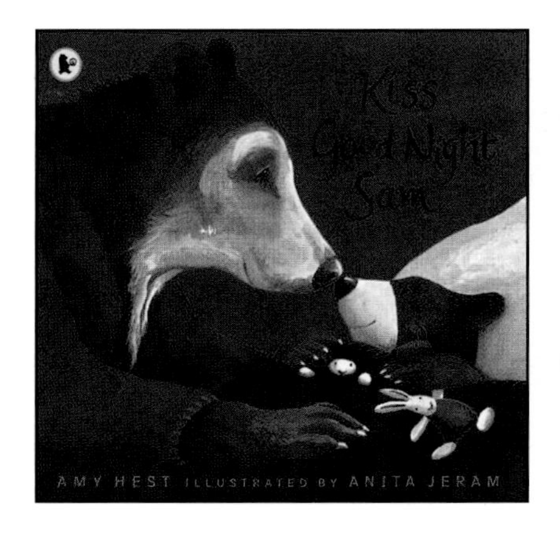

978-0-7445-8935-1

978-1-84428-503-7

978-0-7445-9839-1